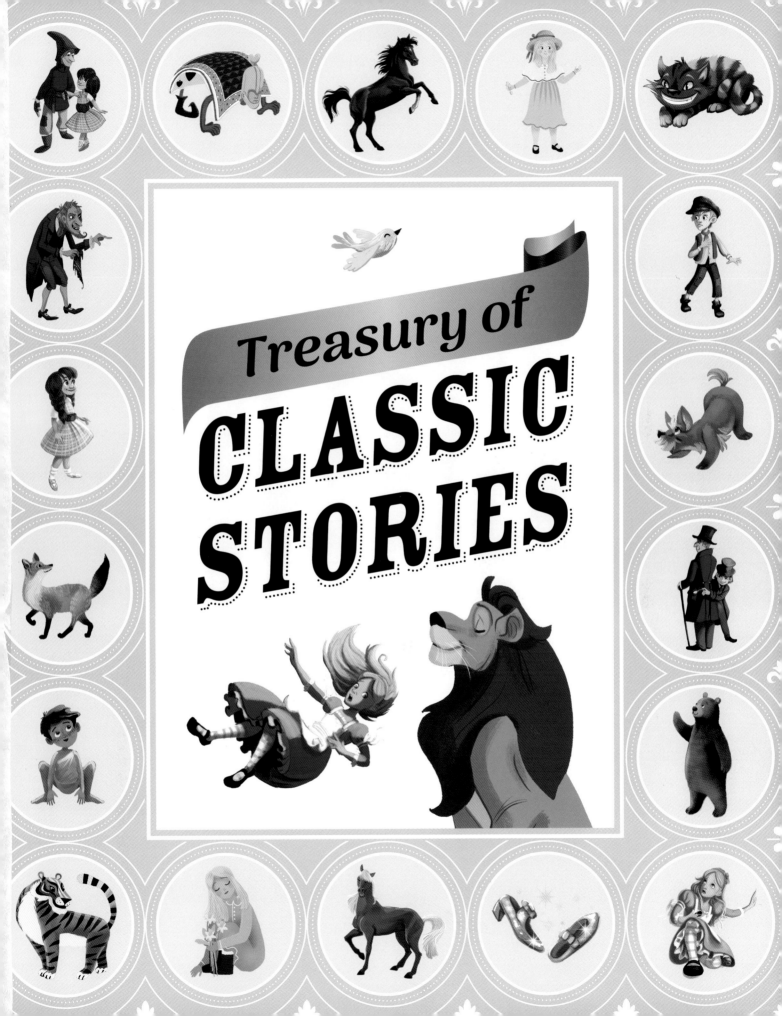

Treasury of
CLASSIC STORIES

This igloo book belongs to:

....

igloobooks

Published in 2019
by Igloo Books Ltd
Cottage Farm
Sywell
NN6 0BJ
www.igloobooks.com

Copyright © 2016 Igloo Books Ltd
Igloo Books is an imprint of Bonnier Books UK

GUA009 0519
2 4 6 8 10 9 7 5 3 1
ISBN 978-1-78905-155-1

Alice in Wonderland
Original story by Lewis Carroll
Retold by Jan Payne
Illustrated by Eva Morales

Black Beauty
Original story by Anna Sewell
Retold by Melanie Joyce
Illustrated by Diane Le Feyer

The Jungle Book
Original story by Rudyard Kipling
Retold by Jenny Woods
Illustrated by Jenny Wren

Oliver Twist
Original story by Charles Dickens
Retold by Stephanie Moss
Illustrated by Eva Morales

The Secret Garden
Original story by Frances Hodgson Burnett
Retold by Melanie Joyce
Illustrated by Jenny Wren

The Wizard of Oz
Original story by L. Frank Baum
Retold by Melanie Joyce
Illustrated by Jacqui Davis

Designed by Justine Ablett
Edited by Hannah Cather & Stephanie Moss

Printed and manufactured in China

Treasury of
CLASSIC STORIES

igloobooks

Contents

Oliver Twist

Black Beauty

The Secret Garden

Alice in Wonderland

One sunny afternoon, Alice and her sister were sitting in the garden. Her sister had her nose in a book and Alice was bored. She was just about to begin making a daisy chain when a white rabbit, with pink eyes, ran past. **"I'm late! I'm late!"** cried the Rabbit. He scurried off across the lawn. **"Oh my ears and whiskers!"** cried the Rabbit, diving down a round, dark hole. **"Wait for me,"** called Alice, running after him. She peered down the hole and, before she knew it...

... Alice felt herself falling. Down, down she went.

Alice landed, **bump**, on a pile of leaves. Ahead, she could just see the White Rabbit disappearing down a long passageway.

She followed him and found a tiny golden key lying on a glass table. The key opened a little door, beyond which was a beautiful garden.

"I'm too big to get through," said Alice.

Then, on the table, she saw a bottle with a label that said, 'drink me'.
"Curiouser and curiouser," whispered Alice. She took a sip from the bottle.

drink me

Suddenly, she began to shrink. Soon, Alice was no bigger than the White Rabbit.

Alice went to open
the door, but found
she had left the
key on the table.

drink me

She cried and cried and soon, Alice was floating in a pool of tears.

"Grab my tail," called a mouse as he swam towards her.
The mouse towed Alice to a safe place on the shore.

After a while, Alice heard the pattering of footsteps as the White Rabbit ran up to her. **"My goodness! I'm late! Oh my fur and whiskers!"** Thinking Alice was his maid, he told her to go into his house and fetch his gloves and fan.

So, Alice went inside the Rabbit's house.

Inside the cottage, a table was laid with
scrumptious things to eat, including
a chocolate cake with the words
'eat me' on it in icing.
Alice cut a piece and
took a large bite.

eat me

Suddenly, she felt herself getting
taller and **taller** and **taller**,
until, with a bump, her head hit the ceiling.

14

The White Rabbit was cross.
**"I have an appointment with
the Queen,"** he said, **"and you
are blocking the door."**

Alice sobbed and, without thinking, fanned herself with the White Rabbit's magic fan.
Immediately, she began to shrink. **"Will I ever be my right size again?"** she wailed.

Alice left the Rabbit's house and walked on. Soon, she heard a sleepy voice, but saw no one, only a mushroom that was about her size. Stretching on tiptoe, Alice peered over the edge and saw a large, blue caterpillar, smoking a strange pipe.

"If you eat two pieces of my special mushroom, one will make you bigger and one will make you smaller," said the Caterpillar.

So, Alice ate one piece of the mushroom and instantly began to gr**OW**. Soon, she was her normal size again.

"I really must go and try to get into the garden," said Alice.

Soon, Alice came to a house where a duchess was sitting by a cat that grinned from ear to ear. **"Why does your cat grin like that?"** asked Alice.
"Because it's a Cheshire Cat," answered the Duchess. **"Now, I must go and play croquet with the Queen."** With that, she hurried away.

Outside, Alice was startled to find the Cheshire Cat grinning at her from a branch. "Cheshire Puss, which way should I go from here?" she asked.

"The March Hare's house is that way," said the Cat. "Do you play croquet with the Queen today?"

"I haven't been invited," replied Alice, but the Cat just smiled and slowly disappeared.

Alice followed the Cheshire Cat's directions until she came to a pretty garden, where the March Hare and the Hatter were taking tea under a tree. Sitting between them, fast asleep, was a dormouse.

"No room!" they cried out, huddling together, when they saw Alice.

"There's plenty of room," said Alice, crossly, and sat down in a large armchair. "How rude," she thought, as the March Hare dipped his watch in a teacup and the Hatter talked in riddles.

The Hatter opened his eyes wide and said, **"Why is a raven like a writing desk?"**
Alice thought and thought about ravens and writing desks.
"Have you guessed the answer yet?" asked the Hatter.
"No, I give up," Alice replied. **"What's the answer?"**
"I haven't the slightest idea," said the Hatter.

Alice was very confused indeed, so she got up and walked off. **"I'll never come here again,"** she said. **"This is the stupidest tea party I've ever been to."**

Alice left the garden and walked back to the woods, just as the Hatter and the March Hare were putting the Dormouse into the teapot.

In the woods, Alice found a door that led back to the glass table with the golden key. Nibbling the second piece of the Caterpillar's mushroom, Alice shrank. Soon, she was small enough to unlock the tiny door and enter the little garden.

There, she found pretty heart-shaped trees and brightly coloured flowers.

Suddenly, a procession came towards Alice and there were shouts of, **"The Queen! The Queen!"** Alice saw the White Rabbit, the Knave of Hearts and then the King and Queen of Hearts.

"Who are you?" asked the Queen.

"Alice, Your Majesty," replied the girl.
"You shall play croquet," commanded the Queen.

Alice thought she had never seen such a curious croquet ground in her life. The croquet balls were live hedgehogs and the mallets, live flamingos.

The card soldiers had to use their hands and feet to make the arches.

The players all played at once, without waiting for turns, quarrelling all the while and fighting for the hedgehogs.

In a very short time, the Queen was in a furious temper and went stamping about and shouting, **"Off with his head!"** about once a minute.

Alice was looking around for some way of escape, when she noticed the Cheshire Cat had appeared.

"How are you getting on?" asked the Cat.

"I don't think they play at all fairly," Alice said, in a rather complaining tone. "They all quarrel and don't seem to have any rules in particular."

"How do you like the Queen?" asked the Cheshire Cat, in a whisper.

"Not at all," replied Alice, tucking her flamingo mallet under her arm and going off to find her hedgehog.

On the way, she met the Duchess and chatted happily to her until someone shouted...

... **"The trial's started!"**

In the courtroom, the King and Queen were seated on their thrones and the Knave of Hearts stood before them. The White Rabbit began to speak...

"The Queen of Hearts,
she made some tarts,
all on a summer's day.
The Knave of Hearts,
he stole those tarts
and took them quite away!"

"Call the witness!" cried the King. Suddenly, Alice had the curious feeling that she was beginning to grOW.

"Alice!" shouted the White Rabbit. Alice jumped up and ran over to the witness stand, tipping it over in the process.

"What do you know about this business?" the King said to Alice.

"Nothing whatsoever," replied Alice.

The King asked the jury to consider their verdict.
"No, no!" cried the Queen. **"Sentence first, verdict afterwards."**

By this time, Alice had grown bigger.

"Stuff and nonsense!"
she said, loudly. **"The idea of having the sentence before the verdict!"**

"Hold your tongue!"
shouted the Queen.

"I won't!" cried Alice.

"Off with her head!" screamed the Queen.

By now, Alice was almost her full size.
"Who cares for you?" she shouted.
"You're nothing but a pack of cards!"

At this, the whole pack rose up and came flying down upon Alice. The cards were soon spinning all around her, so Alice closed her eyes and wished them away.

Suddenly, Alice found herself lying on a bank in the garden.
Her head was in the lap of her sister, who was gently brushing away
some dead leaves that had fluttered down from the trees upon her face.
"Wake up, Alice dear," said her sister. **"It's nearly time for tea."**

"Oh, I've had such a curious dream," said Alice.

She told her sister, as well as she could remember, all the strange and magical things that had happened in her adventure.

When she had finished, Alice got up and ran off, thinking what a wonderful dream it had been.

The Jungle Book

Deep in the jungle, a lost boy sat crying. The sound brought the fierce tiger, Shere Khan, **prowling** through the thick undergrowth. He had chased the boy's parents away and now he had come back for the child.

The tiger was just about to pounce when an enormous bear lumbered into the clearing. **"A man cub!"** gasped Baloo, the bear, in surprise. **"What's your name, child?"**

"Mowgli," said the boy, glancing up at the bear's kind, furry face. **"I know who will look after you,"** said Baloo and he called out to the wolf pack.

Shere Khan **growled** angrily. He had missed this chance to catch the boy, but there would be others.

Soon, Father Wolf and Mother Wolf appeared through the bushes.
"This is Mowgli," said Baloo, nudging the boy forward.

"Poor little cub," said Mother Wolf, giving Mowgli's face a gentle lick.
It tickled so much that he began to giggle.
"Don't worry, Baloo," said Father Wolf. **"We will take good care of him."**

Days later, Mowgli was playing happily with the wolf cubs. Suddenly, a furious **roar** thundered through the jungle and Shere Khan bounded out of the shadows. **"That's my man cub!"** he growled.

Mother Wolf leapt forward. **"Mowgli belongs to our pack now,"** she snapped. **"We will see,"** sneered the tiger, slinking away.

The next time the full moon glowed
in the night sky, Father Wolf took
Mowgli to the pack meeting.

Akela, the leader of the wolves, looked down from his high rock
and asked, **"Why should we allow a man cub into our pack?"**
"Because Mowgli is my cub," answered Father Wolf, proudly.

Baloo held up a huge paw. **"I'll teach him the jungle laws,"** he promised.
Then, Bagheera, the black panther, padded into the ring. **"And I'll watch over him,"** he purred. Akela nodded his head and all the wolves howled together.

Watching from his hiding place, Shere Khan **snarled** with rage.

So it was that Mowgli came to live among the wolves. Baloo taught him the ways of the jungle, and Mowgli would sit and listen to every **rustle** in the grass and every breath of the warm air.

But he would also hear the low **growl** of Shere Khan, as he **prowled** through the trees.

At night, Mowgli heard the **hoot** of owls and the **scratch** of bats roosting in the trees. Soon, even the **splashing** of the little fish in the pools meant more to Mowgli than anything he could remember from his life before the jungle. He was just like any other wolf in the pack.

When Mowgli got bigger and stronger,
Father Wolf taught him how to run and hunt.

Soon, he was as **fast** as any of the pack.

Bagheera showed him how to climb the tallest trees in the jungle. **"This is fun!"**
cried Mowgli, as he **leapt** from branch to branch, following the swift panther.

But Mowgli loved his lessons with Baloo best of all. The bear showed him where to find crunchy nuts and juicy berries...

... and how to ask the bees for their sweet honey.

When Mowgli got too sticky, he **splashed** in the jungle pools and Baloo taught him how to swim.

All the while,
Shere Khan watched...

... and waited.

As the years passed and Akela grew older and weaker, the tiger came to be great friends with the younger wolves. He asked them why they were happy to be led by an old wolf and a man cub.

Bagheera knew how dangerous Shere Khan was and warned Mowgli never to trust him. **"If you are ever in danger, fetch the red flower from the man village, for all animals fear it,"** he said.

The red flower was actually fire, but the animals were too scared to say its name.

After speaking with Bagheera, Mowgli went to find Baloo.
"I'm not scared of Shere Khan," he said, laughing. "I have the whole pack to look after me, and in any case, I'm having too much fun playing with the monkeys."

Baloo warned Mowgli that the monkeys were not to be trusted either, but Mowgli wouldn't listen.

Then, one day, the monkeys **crept** through the trees...

... and **snatched** Mowgli while he was napping.

"Come back!" cried Baloo, but he was too slow.

The monkeys **chattered** noisily and carried Mowgli off to the ruins of the lost city. **"Man used to live here,"** said the monkeys. **"Now, it is ours."**

Meanwhile, Baloo found Bagheera sleeping on a branch.

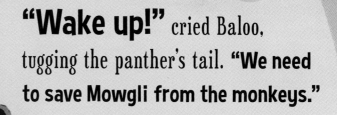

"Wake up!" cried Baloo, tugging the panther's tail. **"We need to save Mowgli from the monkeys."**

Bagheera knew there was only one creature the monkeys were scared of. So, he asked Kaa, the snake, to help rescue the boy.

As Baloo and Bagheera entered the lost city, the monkeys **pounced** on them. Kaa lifted his scaly head and gave a loud **hissss**. Shrieking with fear, the monkeys ran away.

"**Thank you for rescuing me**," said Mowgli, hugging his friends. "**I'll never play with the monkeys again.**"

On the other side of the jungle, Shere Khan was plotting a way to get hold of the man cub. The cunning tiger had persuaded the young wolves that Mowgli did not belong with them.

"Akela is getting older and weaker," he said. **"It is Mowgli who will be leader of the pack when he dies."**

"But if you choose your own leader, you can give Mowgli to me," purred Shere Khan.

"It's true. The boy doesn't belong in the pack," said the young wolves. "He is not one of us."

Father Wolf was hunting nearby. He had heard everything and ran off to warn Mowgli.

Mowgli would not believe Father Wolf. **"Akela is still strong enough to lead the pack,"** he said.

So, Father Wolf took him to watch the hunt. They peered through the leaves as the young wolves called out to their leader, **"Why don't you catch that fine stag, Akela?"**

The old wolf gathered all his strength and **leapt** at the stag. It jumped out of the way and gave Akela a sharp kick.

The other wolves **howled** with laughter, but Mowgli felt sad.

"Akela can no longer protect me," he sighed. **"I know what I must do."**

Mowgli **dashed** through the jungle until he reached the man village. He crept up to one of the huts and peered through the window. Inside, a family was sitting around a fire, talking and laughing together. Every so often, one of them would get up and feed the fire with lumps of charcoal, which glowed in the flames.

Eventually, all of the family went to bed. Mowgli tiptoed inside the hut, quietly took a pot and then scooped some of the glowing coals inside.

Once the pot was full, he slipped out of the hut, looking around to check that no one had woken up.

When he arrived, Mowgli was horrified to see Shere Khan sitting on the high rock, while Akela was slumped on the ground.

As Mowgli left the village, a howl **pierced** through the jungle.

"It is time for the pack meeting," he thought, clutching the pot of hot coals.

"Your leader is a toothless fool!" roared Shere Khan. **"He is doomed to die!"**

Mowgli sprang to his feet. "Does Shere Khan lead the pack? What has a tiger to do with our leadership?"

There were yells of, **"Silence, man cub! Let him speak."**

59

"Give me the man cub," snarled the tiger, "He is a man's child and from the marrow of my bones, I hate him!"

The wolves yelled, "A man! A man! What has a man to do with us? Let him go to his own place."

The young wolves gathered around, **growling** fiercely. Suddenly, Mowgli **jumped** onto the rocks, lifted the pot and threw its contents. The hot coals tumbled out, setting fire to the dry grass. Flames flared up around Shere Khan and he fled into the jungle, **yowling** in terror.

As Mowgli walked away from the fire, he knew it was time for him to leave his forest home. He stopped when he saw his friends. **"It is not safe for me here any more,"** he said, sadly.

"You will be happy in the man village," said Mother Wolf and she licked Mowgli's face to make him laugh.

Mowgli turned to Baloo and Bagheera. **"Goodbye, my friends,"** he said. **"Thank you for taking care of me."**

With a wave and a smile, Mowgli set off towards the village, knowing he would never forget his forest friends.

The Wizard of Oz

Once, on the great Kansas prairies, a girl called Dorothy lived with her Uncle Henry, who was a farmer, Aunt Em, who was his wife, and a little dog called Toto. All around the farmhouse where they lived, as far as the eye could see, was flat, dry, sun-baked earth. One day, a fierce wind came **swirling** from the North. **"Cyclone!"** cried Uncle Henry, running to get the cows from the field. Dorothy grabbed Toto and dashed inside, but the little house **shook** and...

... the terrible wind **lifted** it up as if it were as **light** as a **feather**.

The wind **wailed** and the house **swayed**. Hour after hour passed and Dorothy grew so tired that she lay down and fell asleep.

Then, suddenly, the house landed with a

THUD!

Jumping up, Dorothy flung open the door.
Outside wasn't the dry prairie,
but a beautiful land of tall,
colourful trees, sparkling streams
and pretty flowers.

Out of the trees came a group of people who were the size of children, but looked like grown-ups.

"Welcome to the land of the Munchkins," said a lady with a kind face. **"I am the Witch of the North. You have saved us from the Wicked Witch of the East."**

Dorothy's house had fallen on a witch! All that remained was a pair of silver shoes.

"Oh, dear!" cried Dorothy. "I want to go home to Kansas."

"The Wizard of Oz will help you," said the Witch of the North. "Wear these shoes and follow the yellow brick road to the Emerald City. There, you will find the Wizard."

Dorothy put on the silver shoes and started on her journey.
"Come along, Toto," she said.

They had not gone far when they came upon a scarecrow in a field of golden corn.

"Good day," said the Scarecrow. **"Where are you going?"**

"To see the great Wizard of Oz," replied Dorothy.

"Can he give me a brain?" asked the Scarecrow, for he had a head full of straw.

"I am sure he would," replied Dorothy and they set off together.

Soon they came to a forest, where they found a man made of tin. He was so rusty he could not move.

"This oil will do the trick," said Dorothy, pouring it on the Tin Man's joints. She told him all about the journey to Oz.

"I want to come, too," he said. **"I want the Wizard to give me a heart!"**

So, Dorothy, the Scarecrow and the Tin Man set off into the forest.

Suddenly, there was a ROAR! as a lion bounded out of the trees.

Toto barked and the Lion opened his mouth as if to bite him. **"Don't you dare bite poor little Toto!"** cried Dorothy, slapping the Lion on his nose. **"You're just a big coward."**

The Lion hung his head in shame.
"I know I am," he said. "I guess I was just
born this way. I wish I had courage."

"The Wizard of Oz will give you courage," said Dorothy, who felt
sorry for the cowardly Lion. "You can come with us."

The little group walked for a very long time. At last, they came to a meadow full of poppies. Almost at once, Dorothy and the Lion fell asleep, for the scent of the flowers was poisonous.

"We must move them or they will die," said the Tin Man. **"But the Lion is too heavy."**
"Now we shall never get to Oz," said the Scarecrow.

Then, just by chance, the queen of the field mice came by. She ordered her mice subjects to carry the Lion, while the Tin Man carried Dorothy.

Soon, Dorothy and the Lion were awake again.

"Thank you, Your Majesty," they said.

The friends travelled on and at last they came to the gates of the **dazzling** Emerald City. Everything was green. The houses were green and even the people, too. There was green candy and popcorn, as well as green shoes, green hats and green clothes of all sorts.

The Guardian of the Gates led them through the streets until they came to a big building, exactly in the middle of the city. This was the palace of the great Wizard.

"These visitors wish to see Oz, the Great and Terrible," announced the Guardian.

Inside the palace, Dorothy was taken to the throne room, but all she found there was a giant stone head.

"I am Oz, the Great and Terrible," boomed the head. **"Who are you, and why do you seek me?"**

Dorothy answered, **"I am Dorothy and I want to go back to Kansas. The Scarecrow wants a brain. The Tin Man wants a heart and the Lion, courage,"** she said, earnestly.

"I shall grant all of these wishes, if you kill the Wicked Witch of the West," said the voice.

Dorothy did not want to kill the Witch, but knew that she must.

Now, the Wicked Witch of the West could see great distances. She saw Dorothy and her friends approaching and blew her magic whistle.

The sound sent crows, wolves and bees to torment the travellers, but the Tin Man and the Scarecrow fought them off.

The Witch was so **furious** that she also sent winged monkeys to capture Dorothy and the Lion. The Lion was imprisoned in a cage and Dorothy became the Witch's servant. But what the Wicked Witch really wanted was Dorothy's silver shoes, for she knew they had great power.

However hard the Witch tried to force Dorothy to obey her, though, she would not. So, as punishment, the Witch refused to feed the poor, imprisoned Lion.

After many days, Dorothy became so angry that she **threw** water over the Witch.

"What have you done?" screamed the Witch, angrily. **"Now I shall melt awaaaaay!"**

The Witch did melt and soon disappeared altogether.

Dorothy quickly freed the Lion and, with the Scarecrow and Tin Man, returned at once to the Wizard's palace.

When the group reached the palace's throne room, they heard a loud voice,
"Who are you and why do you seek me?"
"Where are you?" asked Dorothy. "We cannot see anyone!"

ROAR! went the Lion, scaring Toto, who knocked over a screen.

Behind it was a small, grey-haired old man.

"**I am the Wizard,**" said the old man, sheepishly, his voice trembling. "**I will do anything you ask.**"

"**Keep your promises!**" cried Dorothy, sternly.

The Wizard gave the Scarecrow a brain, the Tin Man a heart and the Lion, courage. However, he did not have the power to send Dorothy back to Kansas.

"We can go in a balloon," said the Wizard. **"That is how I came to Oz."** The Wizard busied himself making a big balloon and soon it was ready.

Just as it was about to take off, Toto ran away and Dorothy chased after him.

"Hurry!" cried the Wizard...

... but the balloon floated away.

"Come back!" cried Dorothy. "I want to go, too!"
"Goodbye!" shouted the people of Oz.
The balloon rose further and further into the sky
and that was the last anyone saw of the Wizard,
the Wonderful Wizard of Oz.

"Now I'll never get back to Kansas!" sobbed Dorothy.

"Glinda, the Witch of the South, may help," said the Scarecrow. "The road to her castle is dangerous, but she is your only hope of getting home, Dorothy."

So, once again, the friends set off...

... through **enchanted** forests...

... where the trees seemed to come alive and **fierce** creatures lurked.

At last, they reached Glinda's castle.

"How can I help you, my child?" asked the beautiful Witch.

"My greatest wish is to get back to Kansas," said Dorothy.

Glinda smiled. "Just knock the heels of your shoes together three times and say where you wish to go."

Dorothy hugged and kissed her friends, and said a tearful goodbye.
"Do not worry about us," said the Scarecrow, **"for we shall be very happy in Oz."**

Dorothy held Toto and **clicked** her heels three times. **"Take me home to Aunt Em!"** she cried.

Instantly, she was **whirling** *through the air...*

... until, suddenly, she landed with a big **bump** on the ground. **"I'm in Kansas!"** she cried, looking around.

Aunt Em was running towards her. **"My darling child. Where did you come from?"** she asked, covering the little girl in kisses. **"From the Land of Oz,"** said Dorothy. **"Oh, Aunt Em! I'm so glad to be home again!"**

Here ends the story of the
Wonderful Wizard of Oz.

Oliver Twist

Oliver Twist was born in a workhouse for the poor. **"Let me see him,"** whispered his pretty, young mother. Then, she took her last breath. **"I wonder who she was,"** said the nurse, but the doctor didn't know. Baby Oliver started crying, but if he had known he was all alone, he might have cried even louder.

It was hard growing up in the workhouse, and every mealtime, Oliver and the boys were so hungry that they licked their tiny bowls clean. One day, the others made Oliver ask for more food. Clutching his bowl, he walked up to the front of the hall and said, **"Please, Sir, I want some more."** The master couldn't believe his ears and his face turned bright red!

The owner of the workhouse, Mr Bumble, was outraged. **"Oliver Twist will grow up to be a criminal, I'm sure!"** he said. He decided to get rid of Oliver straightaway and he posted a sign on the door offering five pounds to anyone who would take him.

The next day, the local funeral director arrived at the workhouse.
"Hello, Mr Sowerberry," said Mr Bumble, with a smile on his face.
"Would you like an apprentice?" Mr Sowerberry looked down his
nose when he saw little Oliver, but he agreed.

"Look up, boy," whispered Mr Bumble,
but as Oliver was led away, a single
tear rolled down his cheek.

In his new home, Oliver was only given scraps to eat. **"The dog didn't want these, you little bag of bones,"** said Mr Sowerberry. Hungry Oliver finished every bite and soon, it was time for bed. **"You can sleep with the coffins,"** said Mr Sowerberry. Oliver looked around, feeling scared.

An older boy, called Noah Claypole, worked with Oliver and bullied him.

"Your mother was a bad-un, wasn't she, workhouse boy!" jeered Noah.

"Shut up," whispered Oliver, but Noah refused. Overcome by anger, Oliver grabbed Noah and threw him to the ground.

"Mr Sowerberry!" called Noah. **"He's trying to kill me!"**

Knowing he'd be thrown out onto the streets, Oliver escaped quietly at the break of dawn. He walked for miles, until he saw a sign that read, '70 miles to London'. He'd heard workhouse boys did well in the city. **"I'll go there,"** he thought to himself. **"No one will ever find me."**

He walked on rough country roads for days, eating bread from kind strangers and sleeping in barns. Finally, with aching feet and tattered clothes, he rested in a small street, bustling with people. **"Need somewhere to stay?"** asked a boy with a cheeky glint in his eye, not much older than Oliver.

"I'm Jack Dawkins," said the boy. "Everyone calls me Dodger." Oliver followed him through the filthy London alleys and up some crumbling steps, which led to a dirty room.

Inside, an old man was cooking sausages. "Fagin, this is my new friend," said Dodger. "Come in, my dear," said Fagin.

That night, Oliver slept soundly, but in the morning, he saw Fagin with handfuls of sparkling jewels. Suddenly, he noticed Oliver and whispered, **"What did you see?"** **"Nothing,"** promised Oliver, so Fagin smiled. **"Let's play a game, my dear,"** he said. **"Take this handkerchief out of my pocket without me noticing."**

Oliver was good at Fagin's game, and the next day, Dodger took him on an outing. Before long, Dodger pointed to a smart-looking old gentleman at a bookstall and said, **"That one."**
Then, Oliver watched Dodger take the man's handkerchief from his pocket and run off as quickly as he could.

"My new friends are all crooks," realised poor Oliver.

Then, he heard the police chasing him. **"Stop, thief!"** they cried. Oliver ran, but he tripped and fell on the hard pavement.

Mr Brownlow, the man from the bookstall, said, **"Wait, I don't think this is the boy who did it."**

Mr Brownlow thought he recognised Oliver. **"I must be imagining it,"** he thought, but he wanted to help. So, he asked Oliver to stay with him and the boy was overjoyed.

When Oliver explored Mr Brownlow's house, he saw a portrait of a beautiful woman. **"She looks just like me,"** he gasped.

It was wonderful living with the kind and generous Mr Brownlow, who took better care of Oliver than anyone before. One day, Mr Brownlow asked Oliver to return some books for him. He set off at once, but little did Oliver know, his old friend, Fagin, had not forgotten about him.

"Get him back!" cried Fagin. **"What if he tells the police something that will get us into trouble?"**

So, Bill Sikes, who was a robber in Fagin's gang, told his girlfriend, Nancy, to help them find out where Oliver was.

When their plan was ready, Bill and Nancy set off.

On his way to the bookstall, Oliver heard a woman screaming. Then, she ran towards him.

"Oh, my dear little brother, thank goodness I've found you!" pretended Nancy.

"Come back home," joined in Bill, as his dog, Bullseye, snarled.

"Help, I don't know them!" cried Oliver, as they dragged him away.

Fagin watched Oliver closely for days, but Nancy was kind and grew fond of him.

One night, Sikes grabbed Oliver and dragged him through the dark, foggy streets. **"We've got a job to do,"** he growled. When they reached a grand house, Sikes whispered, **"Climb through that window and unlock the door."**

Oliver realised that Sikes wanted to rob the house and he refused. Then, Sikes pulled out a pistol.

Scared Oliver did as he was told, then suddenly Sikes shouted, **"It's the owners!"** and squeezed the trigger.

There was a

FLASH and a BANG!

Oliver cried out, as his arm started throbbing.

Sikes ran away, but Oliver's arm was hurt and he couldn't keep up. Soon, a sweet voice said, **"It's me, Nancy."** She knew that Sikes and Fagin had planned a robbery, so she had found Mr Brownlow to help Oliver. Then, she had followed the boy to try and keep him safe.

Nancy and Oliver fled into the night, until they saw Mr Brownlow waiting for them at London Bridge. He and Nancy spoke about a man in hushed voices, then Mr Brownlow said, **"I'll find him."** Oliver didn't know who they were talking about, but Nancy hurried away soon after, looking over her shoulder.

Oliver was safe with Mr Brownlow, who took care of his injured arm, but there was still trouble ahead. Fagin had sent one of Dodger's friends to spy on Nancy. **"She snitched on us to that old gentleman,"** the boy told the whole gang.

Sikes was furious and marched home to find Nancy. He slammed the door and locked it behind him. **"Why are you looking at me like that, Bill?"** she whispered. **"You betrayed me!"** he cried, and with that, Sikes raised his fist. Nancy screamed in the darkness, never to be seen again.

Everywhere he went, Sikes was haunted by his dreadful crime. On the run from the police, he heard people whispering as he lurked in the shadows.

"They haven't caught the killer yet," they said, "but the papers say Fagin's been arrested at last. He'll be in prison for life."

With Bullseye yapping at his heels, Sikes was easy to spot, so to escape the police, he climbed up a tumbledown building. Before he could jump to the next roof, someone in the crowd below called, **"There he is!"**

Sikes slipped and fell, finally paying for Nancy's life with his own.

Meanwhile, Mr Brownlow had found the mysterious man he'd spoken to Nancy about. His name was Monks and Mr Brownlow had been his father's oldest friend. He tricked Monks into meeting him so he could find out the truth about Oliver's past. **"I won't turn you in to the police,"** he said, blocking his way. **"Why did you want to ruin Oliver?"**

Monks explained that Oliver was his long-lost half-brother, but he'd asked Fagin to turn him into a criminal. **"Unless he breaks the law, we have to share the money in our father's will,"** he muttered.

Mr Brownlow let Monks go to start a new, honest life. Then, he told Oliver everything.

117

"When I first saw you, Oliver," said Mr Brownlow after dinner, "it was like I knew you." He pointed to the portrait Oliver had noticed before. "My best friend gave me this before he died. Now I know that my friend was your father and the woman in the painting is your mother, Agnes."

Once Oliver knew who he really was, he felt truly happy for the first time in his life. Mr Brownlow taught him to be as bright as he was kind, and he adopted him as his own son. They lived together as a family for the rest of their days.

Black Beauty

My early home, and the first place I can remember well, was a large, pleasant meadow with trees and a pond of clear water in it. I lived with my mother, who was called Duchess. In the daytime I ran by her side, and at night I lay down close to her.

There were some young horses that lived in the meadow, too, but my mother said they were carthorses. **"You are well bred,"** she said. **"I want you to grow to be gentle and not kick or bite."** I never forgot my mother's advice, for she was a wise old horse.

Time passed in that happy place and I grew to be handsome. My coat was soft and glossy black. I had one white foot and a pretty white star on my forehead. Then, when I was four years old, my master said I was to be broken in.

Breaking in meant that I had to
learn to wear a saddle and bridle...

... and to carry on my back
a man, woman or child.

I was to be taught to have a carriage fixed behind me and always
to obey my master's will, without the freedom of my early life.

My training was soon complete, and early that May I was bought by a Squire Gordon and taken to Birtwick Park. At the stables, I was put in a comfortable stall that was clean and airy. Next to me was a fat, grey pony called Merrylegs, who thought himself very handsome indeed.

Across the way was a chestnut mare, looking over from her stall.
Like me, she was about fifteen hands high, but she seemed bad-tempered.
"That's Ginger," said Merrylegs. **"People have been unkind to her, so she snaps and bites sometimes, even though our grooms, John and James, are very kind."**

I soon settled into my new home.
Squire Gordon was a good rider, and
named me Black Beauty because
my coat was dark and shiny.

As time went on, I was put in the carriage with Ginger. She told
me about her early life and how she had been cruelly treated.

I knew it was gentleness that Ginger needed, for I had heard a man say that a bad-tempered master never made a good-tempered horse. With time, Ginger grew much less cross. She and Merrylegs became my dearest friends, and we had many adventures at Birtwick Park.

One stormy day, I was pulling a cart over a flooding river and felt something was wrong. **"Go on, Beauty,"** said my master, but I would not.

"Stop!" shouted a man suddenly.
"The bridge is broken!"
Master said I had saved him and that
animals knew things that their owners did not.

Another time, our master went to town for business and I was stabled there for the night with Ginger. As John settled us down, I noticed a man with a pipe come in.

I thought nothing of it until later, when I saw a red light and a thick, grey cloud across the stalls.

Someone shouted, **"Fire!"** But John spoke gently to me and led me outside.

I whinnied because I could not see Ginger, but at last James brought her out, too. She said that if I had not called to her she would not have had the courage to move.

Soon after that terrible night, James left and a new groom, Joe Green, arrived. He was kind, but inexperienced.

One night, the mistress fell ill and I raced to the doctor's house. I was hot from galloping, so Joe did not put my rug on and I caught a terrible chill.

John looked after me and I soon became well again, but it was not the same for my mistress. Her health was poor, and we soon learned that she and the master were to move to a warmer climate.

I was sold with Ginger to an Earl, and Merrylegs was given to a vicar.

After three happy years at Birtwick Hall, we said a sad goodbye to our old friend Merrylegs, as Joe and John rode us to our new home at Earlshall Park. I held my face close to John's when he left, as that was all I could do to say goodbye.

Earlshall was grander than Birtwick Park, but not as pleasant.
The lady of the house insisted that Ginger and I wore the
bearing rein, which kept our heads high and was uncomfortable.

Ginger kicked out in annoyance and
was never put in the carriage again.

As for me, worse
was to come.

I was cared for by a groom called Reuben Smith. He was a good man, but liked to drink, and this was his downfall. One night when the master was away, he rode me home from town, drunk. There were sharp stones on the road and I lost a shoe, but he forced me to gallop.

I went at such a speed, I stumbled and fell on my knees. I quickly got up, but Reuben was lying on the ground. He groaned, then lay still, for he was dead.

Everyone knew I was not to blame, but my knees were damaged and I needed a long rest.

I was put into a paddock by myself and felt
very lonely, until one day, Ginger arrived.
I was so happy to see her and to have that
time together.

But it was not long after that
I was taken away and sold,
with only a sad whinny of
goodbye to my dear old friend.

In my time after Earlshall, I became a
job horse and was let out to anyone that
wished to hire me. There were many
bad drivers, but some good ones, too.
Because I was patient and good-natured,
one such driver recommended me to a
man called Mr Barry, who became my
new owner.

My master knew little about horses but treated me well.
I would have had an easy time of it, had it not been for one
groom who stole my feeding oats, and another, Alfred Smirk,
who did not clean my stable properly.

My feet became tender and
sore, and I was soon lame.

Mr Barry discovered the truth, and made sure I was fed and cared for. But he was so annoyed at being deceived by the two grooms, he decided not to keep a horse any longer. When my feet were better, I was sold again, this time to a cab driver called Jeremiah Barker.

Jerry, as Jeremiah was known, was a good master and I had never known a family as happy as his. Polly, Jerry's wife, his daughter Dolly and son Harry petted and fussed me. I was stabled with their old white horse, Captain, and we were well looked after.

What a team Jerry and I made, trotting past traffic, through the streets of London. The days were long, but I was happy in my work. Then, one winter, after nights spent waiting in the cold, Jerry fell ill. He was no longer able to work and, sadly, sent me to be sold.

My life as a cab horse after that was very hard indeed. I was so overworked that I became exhausted and ended up at a horse fair. Thin and worn out, I had all but lost hope when I was bought by a kind man called Farmer Thoroughgood.

Even though I was in a poor condition, Farmer Thoroughgood knew
I was well bred. He said that I had seen better days, but with rest
and care, I would soon recover. This was true, for after a winter of
good food and a comfortable stable, I was like my old self again.

When the summer came, Farmer Thoroughgood
said he had found the perfect home for me.
I was carefully groomed until my coat shone.

My mane was combed and
my hooves were painted.

Then, I was taken to a pretty house about a
mile down the road, where three ladies lived.

Miss Blomefield, Miss Ellen and Miss Lavinia were my new owners, and liked me very much. A groom came to feed me and noticed the white star on my forehead and my one white foot.

"Why, it's Black Beauty!"
he cried, for it was Joe Green.

Joe was the best and kindest of grooms, and the ladies promised I would never be sold. I had nothing to fear and, at last, all my troubles were over.

Sometimes, however, I would wake at night and imagine I was still in the orchard at Birtwick Park, standing with my old friends under the apple tree.

The Secret Garden

Mary Lennox was nine years old when her parents died suddenly of cholera. She was sent away from her home in India to live in England with her uncle, Archibald Craven.

He wasn't there to greet her. Instead, Mary was met by Mrs Medlock, who was the housekeeper at Mr Craven's home. She took Mary north to Yorkshire, where Misselthwaite Manor stood on the edge of a wild and untamed moor. Everyone thought she was the most disagreeable-looking girl they had ever seen. It was true, for Mary was a sickly child who had been spoiled all her life by her servants in India. She had thin hair, a thin body and a sour expression.

On her first morning in her new home, Mary woke to the sound of Martha, the housemaid, cleaning the grate. She thought Martha was her servant, and would wash and dress her, but Martha refused. **"Children turn out fools, bein' washed an' dressed an' took out to walk as if they was puppies!"** she said.

At first, Mary was angry. Suddenly, she felt so far away
from everything she knew that she began to cry.

Martha cheered her up by telling her stories of her brother Dickon,
who was twelve and could charm animals. She told Mary about the
moor and the gardens of Misselthwaite Manor.

"One of the gardens is locked," said Martha. "Mr Craven shut it up when his wife died ten years ago. He was so heartbroken, he dug a hole an' buried the key." Mary felt a flicker of interest at the mention of a locked garden. With nothing else to do, she decided she would go outside and look for it.

It was dull and wintry outside the manor.
Mary wandered for a long time through the bare
kitchen gardens until she came to a high, ivy-covered
wall, which seemed to enclose a place on the other side.
There were treetops poking up, and a little robin who
chirruped a friendly greeting.

"Maybe it is the locked garden," thought Mary, "but where is the door?" She ran to ask one of the gardeners, Ben Weatherstaff, where it was. "Don't be meddlesome an' poke your nose where it's no cause to go," he said grumpily, but Mary did not listen.

After that, Mary spent every day outside. Then one morning, it was raining so heavily, she had to stay in. She was busy exploring the corridors of the manor when Mary thought she heard someone crying.

She asked Mrs Medlock about it, but the woman said sharply, **"You never heard any such thing!"** But Mary was sure she had.

The next day it stopped raining, so Mary dashed outside. By the hidden garden, she saw the little robin, hopping about and pecking in the soil. Looking down, she noticed something like a rusty ring of brass or iron. But it was more than a ring. It was a key!

The robin twittered excitedly and a sudden gust of wind blew at the loose curtain of ivy that grew over the wall. There was something behind it and, pushing the ivy aside, Mary saw that it was a door! She slotted in the key and turned it. Mary pushed the door and it creaked open.

At last, she stepped into the secret garden. Inside was the sweetest, most mysterious place anyone could imagine. There were climbing rose stems that grew in tangled trails over the trees and high walls. There were no petals or buds on anything, but it seemed to Mary like being shut out of the world in some fairy place.

Looking at the bare rose bushes, she wondered sadly if the garden was dead. Then, by a shady alcove, she noticed tiny shoots poking up among the yellow grass. **"The garden isn't dead!"** she cried and began pulling up the little weeds. Mary worked until it was time to go inside.

Mary had such red cheeks and bright eyes, and ate such a dinner that Martha was delighted. Mary asked her what might grow in a garden in spring, so she told her all about different types of flowers.

"I wish I had a little spade," said Mary. Martha said she could write to Dickon and he would fetch a tool set from the village.

Some days later, Mary was sneaking to the garden when she noticed a boy of about twelve playing on a wooden flute. His cheeks were as red as poppies and Mary knew at once that he must be Martha's brother. **"I'm Dickon,"** he said. **"I've got th' garden tools."**

Dickon promised to keep Mary's work in the garden a secret. He told her that spring would bring the garden to life, and showed her how to weed with a fork and a hoe.

They worked for hours that day, clearing around the patches of little shoots that pushed up in the wild garden.

After a few days of working in the garden, there was a surprise for Mary. Her uncle, Archibald Craven, had finally returned to the manor and wished to see her. Mary thought he looked stooped and sad, but he spoke kindly. **"I am going away for the summer,"** he said. **"Is there anything that will make you comfortable and happy while I'm gone?"**

Mary felt herself grow brave. **"I would like a piece of earth, to grow seeds in,"** she said. Mr Craven was surprised, but agreed that Mary should choose a piece of earth wherever she wanted to, and be free to run in the fresh air whenever she pleased.

That night Mary was lying awake, thinking about the garden, when she heard the crying noise again. She crept out of her room and followed the sound to a bedroom on the upper floor. There, she found a boy sobbing.

He had a pale, delicate face and large, sad eyes. **"I am Colin, Mr Craven's son,"** sniffed the boy. **"Who are you?"**

"I am Mary Lennox and Mr Craven is my uncle," replied Mary.

"Then we are cousins," said Colin. He said he never went out or saw anyone because he was always ill.

Mary thought Colin a strange boy, but as it rained for a week after their first meeting, she visited him every day. She told him about Dickon and the secret garden, and Colin demanded to see it. He was just like a spoiled little prince, who wanted everyone to do his will and became very angry if they did not.

At last, the rain stopped and the sun shone. Mary raced outside and found Dickon digging in the garden. He had a tame fox called Captain and a crow called Soot. Mary was overjoyed to see her friend and as they worked in the garden that morning, she had never felt such happiness.

But late that night, Mary heard terrible screaming. Racing up to Colin's room, she found him wailing and crying. He was very angry at her for not coming to visit and insisted he would never get well. **"Stop that!"** yelled Mary. **"You are not ill. You just need fresh air and exercise!"**

Mary was the only person who had ever told Colin Craven what to do. Instead of being angry, he listened to her and the next day, Dickon came to take him outside.

Colin breathed the gusts of sweet, fresh air, and as they went into the secret garden...

... the first sight of it made him gasp in delight.

Everywhere, a green covering of tender little
leaves had crept. Trees were laden with
pink and white blossom, and all around
were splashes of purple, gold and white.

Colin stared in wonder. "I **shall** get well," he cried.
"And I shall live forever and ever!"

Mary and Dickon showed Colin around the garden. It was like being in the kingdom of a magic king and queen. Every moment was full of new things and every hour the sunshine grew more golden.

Then suddenly, Ben Weatherstaff's face appeared above the wall.

He had climbed a ladder and was cross to see the children in the garden.
He said Colin was too weak to be outside. Colin's pride was hurt and he
was so angry that he stood right up on his own two feet. Ben Weatherstaff
gasped in amazement and Mary was sure the garden had worked its magic.

The secret garden bloomed and Colin grew stronger. There were eggs in the robin's nest and each day new miracles appeared. Then, one day, Mr Archibald Craven returned to Misselthwaite Manor and to the garden he had locked ten years before. To his amazement, he found his son Colin running and laughing.

"It was the garden that did it," cried Colin, hugging his father. "And Mary and Dickon and the creatures and the magic."

Colin told his father the story of how the secret garden had come alive and how it would never need to be a secret ever again.

Discover all eight enchanting classic tales...

Alice in Wonderland

Join Alice and tumble down the rabbit hole into Wonderland, where nothing is as it seems. This beautiful book is perfect for creating the most magical of storytimes for every little reader.

Black Beauty

Rediscover this moving story of one horse's trials and hardships in this classic tale. When Black Beauty grows to be a handsome stallion, he is passed from one owner to the next, but will he ever be free?

The Jungle Book

Join Mowgli as he learns the strange ways of the jungle, guided wisely by Baloo the bear. This retelling of the timeless classic, with beautiful illustrations, will capture every child's imagination.

Oliver Twist

Delve into the life of pickpocketing crooks in this captivating tale. Follow poor little orphan Oliver all the way from the workhouse until he meets Fagin's gang. Can he escape the streets?

The Secret Garden

Unlock the door to a magical place, full of beauty and mystery. Mary Lennox is lonely and spoilt, but when she discovers a garden hidden in the grounds, it will change her family forever.

Treasure Island

Set sail on a rip-roaring adventure in this classic tale of swashbuckling pirates and hidden treasure. This exciting tale, with stunning original illustrations, is perfect for a thrilling storytime.

The Wind in the Willows

Join Mole and his friends for a riverbank adventure in this classic tale of friendship. Can Mole, Ratty and Badger keep the mischievous Mr Toad out of trouble? Find out in this beautiful, timeless classic.

The Wizard of Oz

Be swept away with Dorothy and Toto to the Land of Oz, where they meet Scarecrow, Tin Man and Lion. This retelling of the well-loved classic story is sure to make storytime exciting.

igloobooks